CLEMENTINES

GREAT BIG
UH-OHs!

By EDIE LAU   Illustrated by FANNY ROCH

CLEMENTINE'S GREAT BIG UH-OHS!

All marketing and publishing rights guaranteed to and reserved by:

FUTURE HORIZONS INC.

Toll-free: 800·489·0727 | Fax: 817·277·2270

www.FHautism.com | info@FHautism.com

Text © 2020 Edie Lau
Illustrations © 2020 Fanny Roch

ISBN: 9781949177527

Every now and again, I come across a book so magnificent, so timely, so wonderful that I find myself wishing with all of my heart that I could magically give it to every parent in the universe.

As a parent, a situation that always stripped my confidence was "What do I do with disappointment?" When my children count on something, want it more than anything in the world and for reasons beyond my control, it goes amiss. I venture and suspect that, like me, you have been there. What makes this so difficult is that when our children suffer disappointment, we suffer as well and we are not only dealing with their disappointment but also ours, too. Helplessness and disappointment, and the fear of how to move forward with a lesson learned rather than a disaster fueled, are not easily navigated in real time.

Although the Clementine series is written for children, you will want to have your own copy that you keep by your bedside when a bad day gets worse, when the storm generates hurricanes and when you've cleaned the house before a family dinner only to discover tomato juice on the carpet.

Clementine, our clever little mouse, inhabits her mother's heart, but she will steal yours, too.

Rachelle K. Sheely, PhD

President and CoFounder of RDI™

Things never seemed to go
the way Clementine expected.

"It's tough being a mouse," she thought.

2

The night before her birthday, Clementine announced,
"There will be no UH-OHs tomorrow!"
She flopped onto her feather bed.
"In fact, my birthday is going to be a day full of
HOORAYS!"

"Sometimes things don't go our way, and that's okay,"
Mama said gently, as she stroked her back.

But Clementine was already
snoring softly.

Clementine woke up bright and early.
"Happy birthday to me!"
she sang.

Joy bubbled in her toes,

wiggled its way through her belly,

then popped like firecrackers
to the tip of her tail!

She scribbled her plans
and got to work.

PLAN
-PREPARE CHEESE
-WHIP UP FROSTING
-MAKE BED

"HOORAY!" she squealed, twirling on her tippy toes.
"My party is going to be perfect!"

6

But when she sliced the cheese,
she spotted mold. HUMPH!
A small pretzel knotted up in her belly.

7

When she spread the frosting on the cupcakes,
she ran out. UGH!
The pretzel in her belly twisted and grew.

Then, Clementine sneezed...

AHHH-CH

OOOO!

... and feathers flew everywhere!

"UH OH!

It's a mess,
and everyone's coming
over right now!" she wailed.

The pretzel in Clementine's belly
twisted into the biggest knot yet.
And it felt like it would last forever.

Clang! Clang! The clock chimed five. Party time!

Five o'clock became 5:01...then 5:02...and 5:03...

At 5:10, Clementine cried, "Did they forget?
OH NO!
My plans are falling apart!"

The pretzel
crunched and groaned
and shook her belly so hard,
she burst into tears.

12

The room was quiet,
except for Clementine's sniffles
and the steady rhythm
of the grandfather clock.

As it ticked and tocked,
Mama hugged her
and hummed along
with the clock:

TICK ONE,
TOCK TWO,
TICK THREE,
TOCK FOUR...

14

After sixty-six ticks and tocks, Clementine wiped her nose.

"I was so scared no one was coming," she sniffled,
"but my UH-OH didn't last that long.
And now everyone's here!"

When it was time for presents, Lulu said,
"This is for all your plans, Clementine!
I decorated it myself!" She giggled.
"Since your UH-OHs have a start and an end,
maybe now you can plan for them!"
"Maybe I can!" Clementine said.

She thought for a moment, then scribbled
on her new chalkboard.
"My UH-OHs can't sneak up on me now!"

18

Everyone sang, "Happy Birthday" and got frosting on their whiskers.

20

TICK ONE,
TOCK TWO,
TICK THREE,
TOCK FOUR...

fter cake, Herbert said, "Let's play tag!"
But Clementine couldn't find the flashlight.
   "Sometimes things don't go my way, and that's okay," she whispered.
      She took a deep breath and hummed with the clock.

PLAN FOR
☑UH OHS

RAY!

After eighty-eight
ticks and tocks,
she found it!

She checked off an UH-OH on her chalkboard.

Everyone raced outside.
Herbert called out, "I'm going to get you!"
Lulu and Clementine giggled and ran
until they were out of breath.

After the tired mice waved goodbye,
Clementine climbed into her cozy bed.
Suddenly, she heard a loud

MEOW

coming from the window!

Clementine opened her mouth to scream,
but she stopped herself. "I'm safe inside."
She dove under the covers and whispered,
"Things might not go my way, but I really am okay."

Just then, Herbert and Lulu jumped out. "Gotcha!"

MEOW

"It's just us!" laughed Lulu.
"We came back to give you a hug.
Sorry we scared you!"
"I wasn't even that scared," Clementine said.
And she really wasn't.

Clementine added BIG UH-OH
to her list and checked that off too.
"Even BIG UH-OHs don't last forever!"

Clementine smiled. "Being a mouse sure is great."

A warm feeling filled her belly,
then zipped down to the tips of her toes.
"I really can face anything!"

Addressing Anxiety

by Jennifer McCaskill, RDI consultant

In *Clementine's Great Big UH-OHs*, Clementine is overwhelmed by feelings of anxiety—until she learns how to recognize and manage them. Just like Clementine, children can be overwhelmed and confused by their feelings. They can become stuck in a cycle of reactivity, leaving them vulnerable even in mildly stressful situations. The fight/flight response within the brain is activated, and thinking shuts down. This pattern is exhausting and can lead to a poor sense of self; when external factors dictate our emotions, we feel powerless.

Parents, caretakers, educators, and therapists can guide children to become more mindful and aware of the rollercoaster of feelings they experience. We can work to build curiosity around feelings, help children to notice them, and then generate meaningful and authentic labels for them. For example, they might classify moments of anxiety as small UH-OHs, big UH-OHs, or even silly UH-OHs. These labels provide greater organization within the brain. Children begin to recognize feelings as information—cues that help them make sense of the world—rather than scary, unpredictable things that just happen to us. Children can also learn to adjust the self-talk that leads to their anxiety. Instead of saying, "Oh no! Everything is ruined!" a child might say, "Sometimes things don't go my way, and that's okay."

When children can find psychological distance from their feelings, they are better able to explore, understand, and manage them. There are creative and respectful ways we can help kids do this. For example, they can play games to practice noticing and even categorizing their feelings of anxiety. They can observe when they feel nervous and where they might feel anxiety in their bodies. We can also encourage children to use different types of media to reflect on their experiences. Just as Clementine records her UH-OHs and hoorays on her blackboard, children can use videos, photos, and drawings to record their own feelings. Exploring and reflecting on their anxiety can help kids feel empowered.

Like Clementine, children can learn to better understand and manage their emotions. As they connect with their internal experiences, a stronger sense of self emerges, story by story.

Clementine's Tips on Becoming an UH-OH Overcomer

by Jennifer McCaskill, Ashlee Moore, and Gabriel and Nathan Lau

Be a Scientist:

An UH-OH is something unexpected that has happened or might happen. If we listen closely to our bodies, we notice that UH-OHs are happening all throughout the day. UH-OHs can be tricky. They can be big or small, long or short. They can be funny or sad, scary or cool.

It's time to put on our lab coats, scientists! Let's conduct UH-OH experiments with our friends and family and see what we discover!

• Throughout the day, when you notice an UH-OH, use a timer to see how long it lasts. At the end of the day, find out who had the longest and shortest UH-OHs.

• Play water balloon toss. Start by standing close to your partner, and gradually step back. As you move farther apart, does your UH-OH feel different? How?

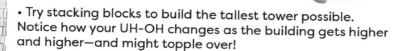

• Try stacking blocks to build the tallest tower possible. Notice how your UH-OH changes as the building gets higher and higher—and might topple over!

Record Your UH-OHs:

Find creative ways to save your UH-OHs: draw tough moments, act out hard situations, or take photos or videos.

Put Discoveries into Action:

Think about how you can use what you've learned from past UH-OHs to face future ones. Use helpful self-talk when an UH-OH shows up. Instead of saying, "OH NO," try saying, "I've got this!" You've gotten through your UH-OHs before, and you can do it again!

Spread the Message:

You learn more about yourself every time you face an UH-OH. Inspire the people around you to overcome their UH-OHs by sharing your own experiences.

DEDICATION

EDIE LAU

For our extraordinary ordinary boys, Gabriel and Nathan. Your hearts are bigger than anyone we know Daddy and I adore you guys.

For our incredible family: Evan Tsao, Rose Cha, Linda Lai-Ling Lau, Chin Kwan Lau, Etai Chen, Joseph Chen, Ivan Chui, Vincent Fu, and especially my beloved mother, Mary Tsao, we love you.

For our outstanding teachers, Lauren Sasaki, Jennifer McCaskill, Jessica Hobson, Jenn Chang, and especially Ashlee Moore, you are our Sunshine every day.

For our people angels: Tasha Dean, Mary Childress, Jessica To, Rommel Sanchez, Alison Weiss, Angie Lew, Juanita Li, Fanny Roch, and especially Tashia Morgridge, thank you for the lifeline.

And for our dearest friends: Sabrina Leong, Shirley Lee, Karie Sedano, and especially Jen Derksen and Joyce Liou, you are like sisters to me; and for my sweetheart husband, SBL, I married up.

FANNY ROCH

For Benjamin, my husband, who supports me every day. For my parents and sisters, who have encouraged me as an illustrator since the beginning. And for my 14 nieces and nephews, who are a wonderful source of inspiration!

EDIE LAU has worked in the field of education in East Palo Alto and Palo Alto for the past twenty years as a teacher and reading/ELD specialist. She also lived and taught in rural and urban schools in Mexico and China for two years.

The loves of her life are her husband and her twin boys. She also cherishes the time she spends with her sweetheart mother, who raised her all on her own, her fun-loving brother, and her hilarious friends. When she isn't laughing with friends and family, she can be found in the kitchen making a mess, attempting to cook while listening to audio books on her phone.

Edie's twin sons, Nathan and Gabriel, have taught her to dance with her UH-OHs instead of allowing herself to be swallowed up by them. "They have inspired Edie to want to help kids overcome their moments of anxiety."

FANNY ROCH studied at Jean Trubert School in Paris. She specializes in illustration for magazine and books for children and illustrated two graphic novels. She also spent three years working for L'Arche, a not-for-profit that provides housing and job training for adults with intellectual disabilities.

She loves being in nature, cooking, sharing meals with her family, and of course drawing and painting! She lives in Nantes, France.

CPSIA information can be obtained
at www.ICGtesting.com
Printed in the USA
LVHW070213100121
676091LV00001B/1

9 781949 177527